Gem & Geson I

Meet Again

GEM & GESON: MEET AGAIN

First edition. November 23, 2023.

ISBN: 979-8227086969

Written by Sweet One.

Written by Sweet One
Translated by Snow Han

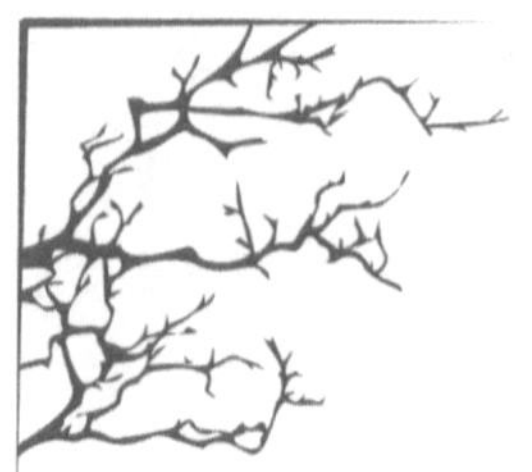

Chapter 1

Pear trees blossomed in Jorleen. The breeze in the early morning blew the dew and the flowers in the Chagon Road into shallow pools left by the heavy rain last night. A male servant, wearing blue clothes and black boots and carrying several silk garments, sneaked into the backyard of the mansion of the Fores.

The Fores well-known in Jorleen had been engaged in tea production and trading through three generations and had owned hundreds of hectares of tea fields outside town and a large number of shops inside town. The head Shangyee Fore used to be a tenant farmer and had made his business prosper since at the age of fifteen he married Miss Rachel Cheng, who was the daughter of a tea trader, and worked with his father-in-law. Rachel was a well-mannered and sensible lady but could not have children, so she let her husband date two other girls: one was Miss Willow whom he met during his business trip and the other was Miss Sallow who was a tenant farmer's daughter and was forced to sleep with him.

Lady Willow was still a peach even in her forties and she had managed the mansion of the Fores since she had three sons. By contrast, Lady Sallow had one son and one daughter but she was not smart enough to gain her position in the family. She died of sadness several years ago.

The male servant in blue clothes was standing in the courtyard where Lady Sallow used to live. It had little sunshine and had no decorations. Bamboo sieves for tea drying were placed at one corner and some fresh tea buds could be seen.

"I'm back, my young lord," the servant said, knocking at the door.

A handsome young man, wearing light green clothes, holding a fan decorated with small paintings of a bridge and a river and framed with carving of willow branches, and with a half piece of white jade carved with moon and peonies tied onto his belt, walked out of the room. He was Gem Fore, the second son of the family. His mother was Lady Sallow and he was disliked by his father, but he was cheerful and clever.

"Have you got the things I want?" the young man asked.

"Yes, including underpants!" the servant Sanbor replied, waggling the clothes. He had been serving Gem for eight years.

Gem nodded and looked at the thin bamboo poles at a corner, and Sanbor knew what to do next. The servant fastened the underpants on one pole and placed it in the gap between stones in the centre of the courtyard and let the underpants flutter in the wind.

"Let's go to see something interesting, Sanbor," Gem said.

The Fores would burn incense and worship their ancestors on the first day and the fifteenth day of each lunar month for a good life and good fortune. Lady Rachel, wearing a purplish grey gown and a golden hairpin, supported by her husband with his hands, walked into the temple. She had been in poor health and had been so vulnerable to colds that she had been staying indoors for the whole winter.

"Good morning, my lady," Lady Willow, resplendent with jewels, said humbly. Her greeting was ignored.

"I'm glad to see both of you," Lady Rachel smiled with a nod, looking at Gem and Lily.

A young, thin girl, standing behind Gem, was Lily, the fifth daughter of the Fores. She and Gem were the children of Lady Sallow.

"Good morning, my lady," Lily said timidly.

"You and Gem may call me auntie," Her Ladyship replied amiably, holding Lily's wrist.

"Rachel has been ignoring me and my three sons but she has been liking the two kids of the dead Sallow," Lady Willow whispered to her husband sourly.

The fifty-four-year-old Shangyee Fore looked like a gentleman but was overcautious and weak-minded, and he owed the good business of the Fores to his father-in-law's competence. Lady Willow had been coveting the family business for her sons since Lady Rachel fell into bad health.

Her Ladyship had been controlling the business of the Fores while Shangyee had had to be a fence-straddler.

He changed the topic and asked, "Where is Jack?"

"He has been preoccupied with work and learning," Lady Willow said loudly on purpose, scowling at her husband, "and he must have burnt the midnight oil studying last night to become a man of knowledge, which was the dream of his father in childhood. He may be too tired to get up early. Shall I wake him up?"

Everybody heard that while Sanbor stifled a laugh but he had to keep quiet after his young master glanced at him.

"Jack has been working hard for our family and he will need more rest," Shangyee responded. He had been favouring Jack.

The solemn ancestral temple of the Fores had a rosewood altar flanked by two wooden armchairs and a horizontal inscribed board with the words "Do Not Scramble for Fame and Fortune" on the beam. That was the family motto left by the late Mr. Cheng who had given his wealth to his daughter and son-in-law and hoped that his offspring could live in harmony rather than in chaos caused by greediness. But fame and fortune would be too inviting to be resisted.

"Come out, Gem!" someone shouted. Everybody saw a man wearing a pink nightgown come in.

Lady Willow sulked.

"What's up?" Gem asked.

The comer, Jack, the eldest son of the Fores, with a pockmarked face and odours of rouge and alcoholic stink overnight, was so cross that he had forgotten the important day.

"I'll kick your ass, son of a bitch!" he cursed, grabbing Gem by the collar.

"Oh, how could you say that?" Gem asked calmly, covering his nose with his fan.

"Don't play dumb! Have you had my clothes taken away?" Jack yelled. "Ms. Gin has told me about it!"

"Who is Ms. Gin, Sanbor?" Gem asked.

"She is the madam of the House of Paradise, which is a brothel!" Sanbor replied at once.

"I've known neither that place nor that woman!" Gem cried out.

"Fuck!" Jack ranted, holding his underpants. "I've left you alone in these years but you have annoyed me! My underpants were in your courtyard. How did you get them?"

Gem stepped backwards disgustedly but kept calm. "Are they yours, Jack?" he asked, lifting the underpants with the handle of his fan and waggling them.

Lady Willow shouted and slapped Jack hard across the face before the latter could punch his younger brother. The man suddenly became sober.

"Mom ..."

"How dare you misbehave in front of your forefathers?" Lady Willow snapped. "Kneel down!" She would have scolded her son much earlier if she had not been stopped by her husband.

"Gem has framed me, dad!" Jack complained bitterly although his mother tried to hold him back. "He had my clothes taken away when I was busy with work, and he would make a fool of me!"

"Were you busy sleeping with a whore?" Shangyee snapped and then walked away.

Lady Rachel watched all this before she left with Lily. Gem saw Lady Willow staring at him fiercely when he stepped over the threshold.

"Have you seen the girls in the House of Paradise, Sanbor?" Gem asked, twirling his fan.

"Yes."

"Were they appealing?"

"Yes, and sexy."

"How?"

Sanbor mimicked those girls' manner of walking while Gem guffawed and ignored the angry woman and left.

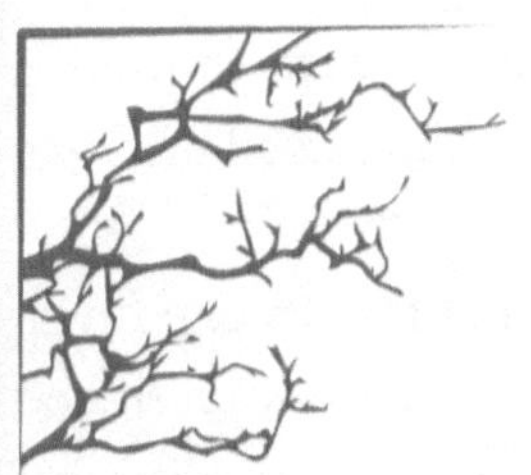

Chapter 2

Jack changed clothes in his room after he was humiliated in front of the temple.

"You should have given a sharp retort to Gem, mom," he complained. "He made me a laughing stock on purpose and dad would not have scolded me if I had been allowed to tell him the truth!"

"Tell me the details now," Lady Willow said calmly, sitting on a sandalwood stool and ready to have tea.

"You asked me to do a part-time job in tea houses. The ministry councillor Mr. Sun came to town and would buy some aged tea. I wanted to seize the hard-to-get opportunity and raise prices, so I invited him to have fun in the House of Paradise. But I could not find my clothes including my underpants after I woke up!"

He was thumping the table angrily.

"How did you know that it had been done by Gem?" his mother asked.

"Ms. Gin told me. I was so furious that I would punch him, but I saw my underpants hanging on a bamboo pole. That must have been done by him, too!"

"Did Ms. Gin tell you about it?" she asked doubtfully.

"Yes."

"What did she say?"

"She said that Gem had his servant Sanbor threaten her. He broke in and made off with my clothes and humiliated me as an impetuous incompetent!"

"You are stupid!" she shouted, smacking the tea cup down on the table. "I've told you that you should behave yourself and learn how to get along with others. But even a procuress has refused to help you! How can I support you to scramble for the property of the Fores?"

"Ms. Gin helped me and told me about the whole thing," he retorted.

"You are an idiot! Your father is just a businessman, not a high official. How could Sanbor, Gem's servant, enter the House of Paradise at will and take away your clothes when there were security guards? Gem is a frequent visitor to the markets of flowers, birds, and aquatic products, and he is praised as a good man. He is smarter than you. Perhaps he has colluded with Ms. Gin to infuriate you and make you a laughing stock in the temple!"

He was confused but soon he realised that something must have been wrong. Ms. Gin, the madam of a brothel, should have kept it secret if one of her customers had lost his belongings in her house. But she told him in the early morning that his clothes had been stolen and then gave him a pink nightgown. Why?

He gnashed his teeth and was about to leave.

"What are you going to do?" his mother asked.

"I'll kick Gem's ass!"

"You are such a foolish, impetuous boy!" she snapped, grabbing him by the ear. "Gem will ensnare and destroy you after I die!"

"But I must fight back!" he shouted.

"Gem is a cunning man under the mask of a good man. He has embarrassed you in public and he will do much more."

"What do you mean?"

"He did not throw a stone at you until Rachel showed up. Has he been coveting the family wealth?"

"That's right. But he can't do anything with his sick sister."

She started to think about Lily instead of arguing with her son. Lily was the only daughter of the Fores. Her father did not love her mother but had hired a tutor to teach her knowledge and art since her childhood, and he hoped that she would become a refined lady.

Gem and Lily had a talk with Lady Rachel and then came to a pavilion in an artistically designed backyard which was built by their father, a great lover of horticulture. Gem appreciated the bonsai nurtured by himself for so long.

"New branches from the Sageretia theezans?" Lily asked.

"Yes," Gem replied. "It is a shade-enduring plant and enjoys sunshine and its roots can grow fast. The pot should be large inside with more soil and be eye-catching outside and should be changed often. And the soil should be loosened frequently. All in all, it is a difficult job."

She made tea for him. "It is not easy but you have been taking care of it for so many years," she said smilingly. "You do like it."

"Indeed." The bonsai resembling an emerald was an elaborate thing for Gem.

She gave a white porcelain cup patterned with vines to him and enjoyed sightseeing with him, but she grew absent-minded.

"Do you like the bonsai?" he asked, tapping the stone table with his two fingers.

"You like it and I like it, too," she replied nervously.

"It's yours now."

"But you have been nourishing it for five years."

"You have been my younger sister for sixteen years. The bonsai is a gift to you."

"Thank you very much. I ..."

"What's up?"

"Nothing."

"Just tell me."

"I ... I'd like to know ..." she stammered, blushing.

"About Konlin, right?"

The girl looked like a red rose.

Konlin was the son of a tenant farmer who had been renting the tea fields of the Fores. He was attracted by Lily who was watching fish by the lake when he was just a little boy and came to the mansion of the Fores to pay the rent. Since then love had grown and they had been able to meet each other only once a month because of the gap between them. But she had been worried about Konlin since he did not show up this month.

"What has happened to him?" she asked anxiously.

"He gave me new tea the other day," he replied, sipping his tea.

"He should have seen me when he came here."

"He asked me to keep you in the dark."

"But why?"

"Because his father would have him marry another girl."

Lily became speechless and looked pale.

"Don't worry. Konlin has been so faithful to you that he has said no to that girl. But ..."

"Say it!"

"You and Konlin have reached marriageable age," he said, putting down the cup and looking at his uneasy sister. "Our father will have you marry another man if Konlin does not bring up proposal of marriage."

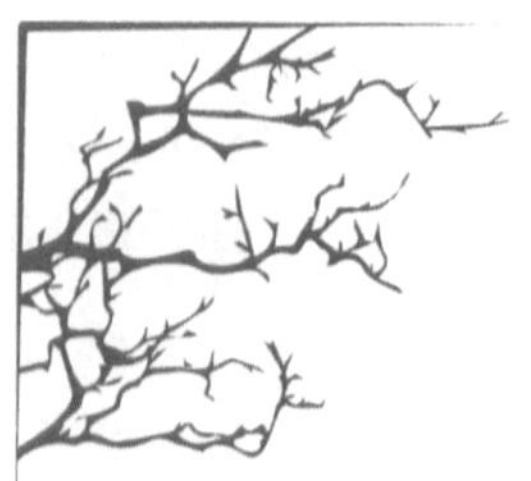

Chapter 3

Lily's soon-to-be-husband, who came from the prestigious Fang family in Chuchou, was chosen after half a month.

Good word of mouth was important to both bonsai and tea. There were four well-known families engaged in tea production and trading: the Fangs in Chuchou, the Taos in Yichou, the Hus in Mingchou, and the Fores in Gingchou. The Fangs were the top and provided tea and rice for the aristocrats. The eloquent Lady Willow chose a good husband for Lily and would have her marry Geson Fang, the head of the Fangs. Everybody knew, however, that Geson had been sitting in a wheelchair for over a decade since he became crippled in an accident, and he might be impotent.

A bamboo-braided lamp was hanging in front of a narrow door at night while fragrance of tea was permeating the air. Bamboo clips, bamboo teaware, and a roller with tea crumbs were placed on the floor.

Gem had been engrossed in playing chess alone since he had lunch today. He used the white chess pieces with his left hand and the black ones with right hand. He started to feel cold after several hours had passed, but the final result was yet to come.

"It's time to sleep, my young lord," Sanbor said, holding a hot cup of tea.

"Wait a minute," Gem said, too absorbed to sleep.

"The cooking team members said even Lady Rachel had agreed with Miss Lily's marriage," Sanbor continued. "Her Ladyship should have protected your sister from the pit of hell."

He failed to persuade Gem to sleep early but prattled on about the marriage. "It is said that Geson Fang, the head of the Fangs, is a moody, mad, and foolish weirdo. Their family business has fallen into decline and your sister's life will be ruined if she marries him. Lady Willow is too wicked."

The Fangs used to call the shots and keep up good relations with the other families through tea tasting events. They had, however, been locking themselves in their mansion and had been losing their prominence since Geson started to lead their family. A lame man preferred to stay indoors.

"Have you ever met Mr. Geson Fang, my young lord?" Sanbor asked.

"Yes, in my childhood."

"Was he a bad guy like rumours said?"

"Rumours are not true," Gem said, holding a black chess piece.

"I don't give a hoot about Mr. Geson Fang's health condition if the bride is someone else, my young lord," Sanbor continued. "But your younger sister, who has been deeply in love with another man, will be forced to marry Geson. Don't you know how sad she is?"

Someone was walking outside. Sanbor went out holding a lantern without asking any question. Few people knew the back door of the mansion of the Fores and few visitors would come here at midnight. The comer must be Konlin who had learned of the arranged marriage and would need help.

Sanbor opened the door and saw the plainly-dressed, tall Konlin. The latter nodded to the former and then walked towards Gem quickly. The young lord let the man sit down.

"Why do you come here late at night?" Gem asked, sipping his tea.

"I ... I'm ... still worried, sir," Konlin stammered.

"About what?" the young master asked, putting a black piece on the chessboard.

"My father did not have a matchmaker find a good girl for me," Konlin replied anxiously. "But you told Lily that my father had done that. Would she get so angry that she might marry the lame Geson Fang?"

"Do you doubt my sister's affections for you?" Gem asked.

"No! Even though she and I are ..."

"Faithful to each other."

"What should I do if she were forced to marry that man?" Konlin cried out, holding back his tears.

"Go home now and she will be with you soon," Gem said, giving a handkerchief to him. "You must cherish her and let her take good care of the bonsai." And then he entered his own room.

"When did my young master tell you about the arranged marriage of his sister?" Sanbor asked in puzzlement.

"Before the Spring Festival," Konlin replied.

"Really?" Sanbor cried out in surprise. "But I did not know that at all!"

"He asked me to get ready to elope with Lily," Konlin said with hidden happiness.

Sanbor was still puzzled after Konlin left. He came from an impoverished family and became a beggar, and he got caught by Gem one day when he was so hungry that he tried to steal some steamed bread. Later he served Gem and since then he had understood his master quite a lot. But now he could not figure out his master's plan.

Gem had embarrassed Lady Willow and her son in the ancestral temple, so she chose a handicapped man to be Lily's husband to get even with the girl's brother. Konlin said, however, that Gem had thought of the woman's scheme before the Spring Festival. Was Gem a fortune teller? Did Gem infuriate Lady Willow intentionally so that he could let Konlin and Lily be together even though they could not have a wedding ceremony? Lily would have to have an arranged marriage sooner or later. Gem made up a story that Konlin's father had had a matchmaker choose a girl for his son so that Lily would be determined to elope with Konlin. All this was Sanbor's thinking, and he admired his master's wisdom and consideration for his younger sister. He rushed into the room and would tell Gem that he was blessed to serve such a good master as him and would always be loyal to him, but he was so astonished that he fell over when he saw his master.

"What are you doing, my young lord?" Sanbor asked at the sight of mirror and rouge, getting to his feet.

"I'm putting on my makeup, for practice now." Gem said calmly.

"But why?"

"I'll be the bride."

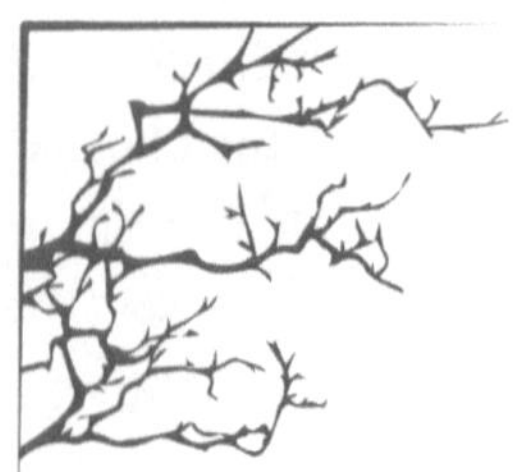

Chapter 4

After five days, a servant said that Miss Lily had been gone, leaving only one letter.

The girl's father was pacing the courtyard nervously while Lady Rachel was sitting in the important position and reading the letter.

"What should we do?" Lady Willow said hypocritically, sipping her tea leisurely in the less important position. "The betrothal presents of the Fangs will soon arrive here. They cannot be offended even though their influence has been declining."

"It's your fault, Willow!" Shangyee cried out. "You should not have rushed to find a husband for Lily!"

Lady Willow wanted to thump the table but had to subdue her anger when Lady Rachel was still sitting nearby. "I would not have taken great efforts to contact the Fangs if you had not agreed with it, and I hoped that your daughter could have a happy marriage. You should not have blamed me for her elopement."

Shangyee became speechless. He allowed Lady Willow to find a good husband for Lily, but he had never thought that his lovely daughter should elope with the guy who was the son of a poor farmer.

"Did you know that Lily had had a sweetheart?" he asked.

"Yes."

"What you had done has forced Lily to go!"

"She should have had a good, rich husband," Lady Willow cried. "I am not your punching bag!"

"Oh, I'm sorry," he said awkwardly. He always scapegoated others.

Gem was asked to come up with a solution but he was enjoying himself in the drawing room. "Your younger sister has run away from home but you are still careless of that!" his father snapped.

"Shall I find her?" he said, looking at Lady Willow.

"You don't have to do that," she said after a moment of consideration. "I've had servants search for her, and you will stay at home and wait for news of her. But we must have a substitute for her if we can't find her."

"Who can be the substitute?" Shangyee yelled.

"We only have one daughter," Lady Willow said unctuously. "Things would get worse if we chose an outsider. Oh, I remember that you and Geson were childhood friends, Gem."

"That's right," Gem said.

"Both of you were such good friends!" Lady Willow said, gnashing her teeth. She clearly remembered that the two naughty kids threw Jack into a river. Geson helped Gem get her Achilles' heel and since then Gem had put her in the dry tree for so many years. It served them right that Geson had been crippled and Gem had been disliked by his father.

"Gem had seen Geson on tea tasting events," Shangyee said. "The two boys played with pets and led Lily onto roofs and trees."

"They were just kids," Lady Willow added sanctimoniously. "For their childhood friendship, let Gem sit in the bridal sedan chair if Lily can't be found."

"Let Gem be the bride?" the husband asked.

"Yes," she explained. "There must be a bride. Gem and Geson used to be good friends, and things can be made clear after Gem arrives at the mansion of the Fangs. If the chair were empty, the Fores would be criticised for disregarding the prestigious Fang family after the old Mr. Fang passed away. We should not fall victim to a pretext for gossip."

"What will come after the wedding ceremony held by Gem and Geson?" he asked hesitatingly.

"Geson can divorce Gem later," she said carelessly.

"That would be an embarrassment!" he retorted angrily.

"Let Gem come up with a solution," she said lightly.

Shangyee became speechless and he was still concerned about his son's marriage although he disliked him.

"I should do something for our family regardless of the result and I will obey my father and Lady Rachel," Gem said kindly at the sight of his father's hesitation.

Shangyee had to listen to Lady Rachel. The latter put down the letter and asked Gem to come to her room and then had a maid serve tea.

"You are a smart boy, Gem," Her Ladyship said kindly, tapping his forehead.

"Really?" he asked wittily.

"You have been thinking about someone else when you are living in our house."

"I just want to do the right thing."

"To be Geson's bride?"

"Oh, he is a cold, desperate weirdo."

"I feel pity for Geson and I wonder if he can still remember your happy days in childhood after so many years have passed," Her Ladyship said with a sigh.

"Those days have been engraved upon my heart, and that's the most important thing."

"You have played a trick on Willow. She intended to drive you away but she has been fooled by you. What's more, she has spent all her money contacting the Fangs."

"But she has facilitated my plan."

"How?"

"She is astute and jealous of others' good life and has been itching to throw me out. She used Lily's marriage as a pretext and chose the disabled Geson of the declining Fangs as the worst husband for Lily. What's more, she foreknew that my younger sister would elope with Konlin, and at last she would let me be the bride."

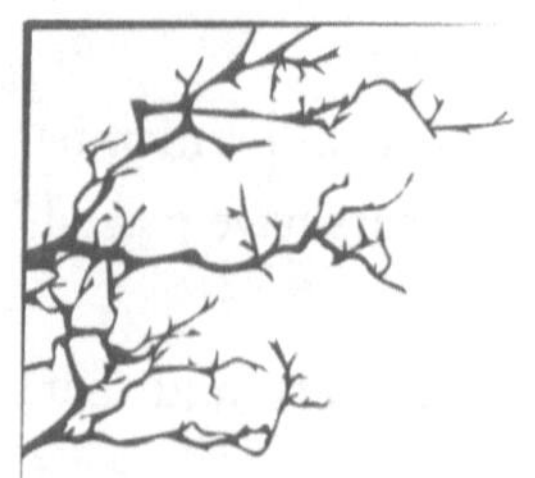

Chapter 5

Lady Willow persuaded her husband to let Gem be the bride if Lily could not be found, and she said that Geson Fang must not divorce Gem so that the reputation of the Fores could be upheld.

One memorial tablet of the late Mr. Cheng was placed on the altar of the ancestral temple. The Fores, which had less than twenty members, would have Gem marry Geson Fang and would not allow him to return for the sake of the family honour.

Stevedores resumed their work after several days of rest because of too much rain in spring. A thin, bouncy man in his fifties with a slight stoop came to the riverside three days in a row, and he would watch the ships and wait for someone after he arrived. The river was sourced from an area 20 miles outside Chuchou and it was a convenient transportation hub for business and passengers.

"Are you waiting for the bride, Uncle Mute?" a boatman asked, holding a tobacco pipe and walking towards the old man. The latter nodded and then pointed at the sky and the berthing ships.

The boatman understood him. "The bride may arrive soon," he said. "Many ships from Jorleen have been delayed because of the bad weather."

Uncle Mute smiled at him and gave him two coins. Later he went to a tailor's shop in the South Street and bought new clothes, and then he went to the North Street and bought a bag of sweet fried sesame balls.

"These rice balls have a lot of sugar and Mr. Geson Fang will like them," the bakery keeper with an oily apron on his waist smiled, looking at Uncle Mute.

The elderly man gesticulated to express his thanks with clasped hands to the keeper and then went on with walking until he stopped in front of a mansion.

The front gate of the mansion of the Fangs was opened just before ten o'clock in the morning. The two guards yawned and stood there lazily. One of them was Jim and he stopped Uncle Mute from entering the house.

"Where have you been?" Jim asked rudely, "And what have you bought?"

Uncle Mute gave the things to him. Jim tore open the box and took out a new cloak. "The cripple will waste the cloak if he wears it," he sneered. And then he opened the bag of the sweet fried sesame balls without permission and put one ball into his mouth and then spat it out. "Fuck! It's shit!" he cursed. The sharp-eyed Uncle Mute snatched the clothes and the food and squatted as though he picked them up just before Jim threw them.

A servant named Robert said something to Jim and looked at Uncle Mute and hinted that he should go into the house at once.

"Her Ladyship should have driven away the disabled man and the old man," Jim bawled, spitting at Uncle Mute's shadow, "and the Fangs should have a new leader."

That was nothing new to Robert although he was just a new servant in the Fang family. "Uncle Mute has been working for Mr. Geson Fang," he said after a moment of consideration, "and we should ..."

"The Fang family will have a new leader," Jim interrupted, looking at the plaque and gloating.

The Fores had a lavishly decorated courtyard but the Fangs had a plainly but distinctively one. Uncle Mute carrying the things entered the lush courtyard. Birdcages were hanging on cassia trees and door lintels were carved with auspicious birds and wintersweet, but the carvings were dusty because of infrequent cleaning. He could not speak so he knocked at the door but no one answered. He walked inside and put down the clothes in the bedroom and then put the sweet fried sesame balls on a white jade plate.

The wedding ceremony would be held soon but the Fangs only made a perfunctory effort. Two red lanterns were hanging at the entrance of the mansion and there was no more festive decoration. Uncle Mute paced the drawing room nervously and did not know on which table he should put the plate down.

The sweet fried sesame balls had been prepared for the special guest whose seat was still uncertain. The guest was the brother of the bride and might come here. Uncle Mute could not decide, so he went into the study.

A handsome man with a black string tied at the end of his long loose hair wearing a dark robe was sitting at a desk and touching a half piece of white jade which was carved with a lovely bird standing on a flower and which had been worn by him for so many years. He was the crippled Geson, the head of the Fangs. He heard Uncle Mute entering his room and saw him holding a plate and gesticulating: the bride would soon arrive.

Geson put the jade into a lock box and calmed down after he watched it for a long moment of inner turmoil. "He is fond of sweet food and will have it no matter where it is put," he said lightly.

Robert said loudly that the bridal procession of the Fores would soon get here from Jorleen and Mr. Geson should put on his wedding garment and attend the ceremony.

The journey lasted for nearly half a month. Sanbor holding a tree trunk vomited as soon as he went ashore instead of supporting Gem wearing a wedding dress to sit in the bridal sedan chair. Jack, who had been forced to join the team, was annoyed but he started to smirk at the thought of seeing Gem no more from then on and even became excited when he was sitting in the carriage pulled by the poor old horses provided by the Fangs.

"We should run away now to protect ourselves from the scheme of the cunning Lady Willow, my young lord!" Sanbor whispered, walking beside the sedan chair and carrying baggage.

Gem remained silent.

"Let's act at once," his servant continued nervously. "The witch perhaps has colluded with the Fangs, and we must avoid the trap!"

Gem tapped Sanbor on the forehead with his fan.

"Will we go or not?" Sanbor grumbled. "Things will get worse if we live in the mansion of the Fangs. Playing tricks on Jack will be much better than that."

"I'll live with my husband," Gem said smilingly, lifting the red bridal veil.

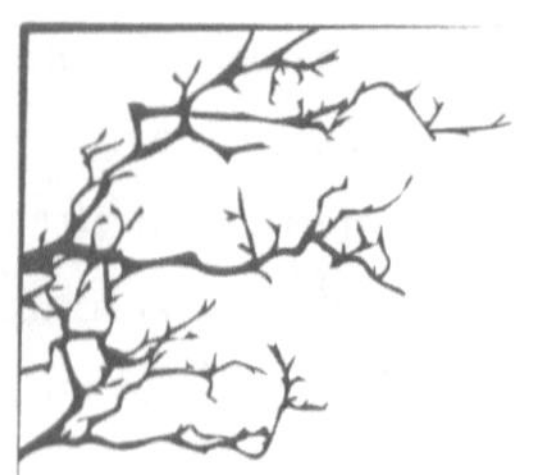

Chapter 6

A wedding ceremony should be joyous but it was like a funeral in the Fang family. The bride Gem was asked to step over a special brazier, a part of the ceremony, just after a long journey. Sanbor supported the bride with his hands and walked into the drawing room and saw a noble lady named Wong sitting in the important position.

The woman was neither Geson's mother nor the wife of the late Mr. Choron Fang. She used to be one of the distant relatives of the Fangs and had had a head for figures since her childhood. Choron had her manage dozens of tea houses and since he died she had been responsible for all the accounts. She was Lady Shrewdning Wong, the actual leader of the Fang family.

"Welcome to the Fang family, Gem," she said insincerely. "I've been taking care of Geson since his parents passed away. Today, on behalf of his parents, I hope that you will have a happy life with him."

"You are a kind-hearted, beautiful parent, madam," Gem replied. His sweet talk was pleasing Lady Shrewdning while Geson wearing a black cloak showed up in his wheelchair.

"Mr. Geson is appealing," Sanbor murmured.

"A lovely kid has become a hunk," Gem whispered proudly.

"Huh?"

"What?"

"He is looking for something," Sanbor said. He saw emotional changes in Geson's eyes: expectation, sadness, and calmness.

"The couple will have nuptial wine and worship gods and have three kowtows!" someone yelled. Gem was jostled into the bridal chamber before he could get more information about the bridegroom.

No friend or guest came to attend the poor wedding ceremony which even had no firecrackers. Gem had had no food or water for a whole day and had been waiting for his husband in the room for five hours, and he was so ravenous that he lifted the red bridal veil.

"I wanted to give you a big surprise, Geson, but you have left me alone here," he said peevishly.

After he walked into the drawing room, he glanced at the lotus nuts and peanuts on the table and then saw the sweet fried sesame balls which he used to have many years ago.

"Geson still has a fondness for them," he talked to himself happily. He chewed one ball but had to have tea at once. "Ah, it's too sweet!" he exclaimed.

He had two sesame balls and still remembered that Geson loved them and he had them together with him when they were just kids.

Shadows of lamps were flickering outside and cool breezes were blowing. A servant said that his master should go to sleep. Gem holding a sesame ball walked into the courtyard and saw one man standing beside a seated man under a cassia tree.

"Geson!" he said cheerfully.

He turned around after a long moment of silence and motionlessness.

"Why are you here, Gem?" he asked in astonishment.

"I'm here for you although you didn't want to see me," the bride replied delightedly, chewing an excessively sweet sesame ball.

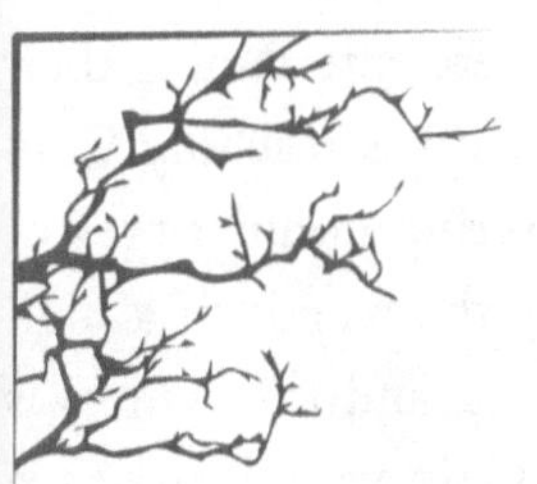

Chapter 7

Gem and Geson had been childhood friends. They met each other for the very first time in Mount Yumin, Chuchou during the tea tasting event which was held every five years and would last for more than two weeks each time. Just after the Fores were recognised as one of the four prestigious families engaged in tea production, Mr. Choron Fang invited Mr. Shangyee Fore and his wife Lady Rachel to take part in the event.

Lady Sallow was alive but weak and gloomy at that time. Lady Rachel took good care of her and her son Gem, a thin, seven-year-old boy who was often bullied by Jack. Before the couple started their journey to Mount Yumin, Gem was so badly beaten up by Jack that their father punished the attacker with a cudgel. Jack wailed and said that he had been wronged because he had just pushed Gem but did not batter him.

Shangyee was not a sensible man and he blindly believed what he had seen, so he spanked Jack much more. Lady Rachel watched them and then went to her bedroom and saw Gem, who was safe and sound and had removed the red pigments from his face, applying her cream to his cheeks.

She wanted to have a talk with him but decided to take him to the tea tasting event to avoid another brawl between him and Jack. Lady Willow, however, considered that Her Ladyship favoured Gem and since then her grudges had increased.

When Choron and his wife Orchid were entertaining their guests in the Mount Yumin, Lady Rachel was teaching Gem different methods of brewing tea: Showering meant rinses of tea ware, and Pour High meant holding the teapot in a high position and pouring boiled water; a long and thin cup was Fragrance Cup, and a well-proportioned cup would make tea liquid smooth.

The naughty Gem played with flowers and plants so curiously that he forgot the knowledge and skills about making tea taught to him by Lady Rachel and fudged Shangyee's questions. The father got so annoyed that he asked his son to stand nearby a pavilion at the top of a hill as a punishment.

Gem kicked stones and enjoyed himself immensely. One of them rolled and stopped beside a pair of black boots. He saw a boy smiling at him in the breeze. That boy was the captivating Geson Fang.

"What are you doing here?" Geson asked.

"I was asked to stand here as a punishment," Gem replied.

"Why?"

"Because I failed to answer my father's questions and I embarrassed him in public."

"I can teach you to recognise different kinds of tea."

"Who are you? And why do you want to teach me?"

"I'm Geson Fang."

"Are you the son of the Fangs?"

"Yes," Geson said tenderly, grasping Gem's wrist. "Let's go. It's windy here. You will not be scolded by your father if you are with me."

Gem followed him but suddenly he freed himself from Geson's grip and ran backwards. Geson was surprised but chased after him.

Four or five superior tea bricks together with a shovel were put on the ground behind the pavilion and they would be buried into the newly dug hole.

"Well, there must be a scheme beneath your smile," Gem said derisively, glancing at Geson.

The boy looked serious at once.

"Lady Rachel has told me that Geson Fang is well-mannered but poker-faced," Gem said.

"I can be smiling, and I can be cool."

"I've never seen you. But why did you smile at me?"

"I did that because I thought that you were a good boy."

"You had your plan."

Geson's plan failed and he had to continue with shovelling earth.

"This is Floating Clouds, the brand created by the Taos," Gem exclaimed in astonishment, squatting and picking up one tea brick.

"Do you know it?" Geson asked.

"Yes," Gem said proudly. "Its texture is winding and it looks like clouds or fog. It has a mellow and lingering flavour after it is brewed with mountain spring water. Only the Lotusherb made by your family can be comparable to its superiority. Lady Rachel said the two kinds of tea were different, but I think the Lotusherb is much better and has an extremely rare tea liquid colour and good mouthfeel."

Geson put down the shovel and sized up Gem again. "You are knowledgeable and you should not have embarrassed your father in public," he said.

"I'm willing to let him down because he has never treated me as his own son and has never loved me," Gem replied unhappily at the thought of his sorrowful mother and his cold-blooded father. "Well, let's change the topic. Even one piece of the Floating Clouds will be lucrative, and there are other tea brands, such as Maples and Tenderain. What will you do?"

"I'll bury these tea bricks lest my father should have me taste the tea in front of everybody again," Geson said. "I've been fed up with that and I don't want to be a toy for display anymore."

"Ha ha! I'm fond of such a charming toy as you!" Gem exclaimed freely.

The listener blushed at once and went on with burying the tea bricks.

"Mr. Geson!" someone shouted. The boy threw the shovel and, grasping Gem's hand, ran.

"You can run alone and let me go," Gem said in a hurry.

"You saw my deed just now," the other boy retorted. "What if you might betray me?"

"I am a man of integrity."

"That may not be true. Let's walk down the hill now."

"It is my first time here in Chuchou, and I don't want to get lost!"

"Don't worry. We are in our family's turf and I'll be your guide."

The two boys enjoyed themselves in their little world but they were scolded by their parents after they were found by them after two weeks. Before they went home, they said that they would have fun in the lake and watch lanterns together in the next tea tasting event.

Later Geson and his father would visit the Fores whenever they went to Jorleen. Gem thought that Geson would be his best friend in his life, but his connection with his buddy had been suspended since an accident happened in the Fangs, leaving him with unanswered letters and refusals of entrance.

Gem was engulfed with thoughts and questions but saw Geson sitting in his wheelchair blankly, looking astonished and worried, and stifling his delight. Gem had to shrug because he did not know where to start.

"It's getting cold, Geson," he said after some hesitation. "You'd better go to sleep now."

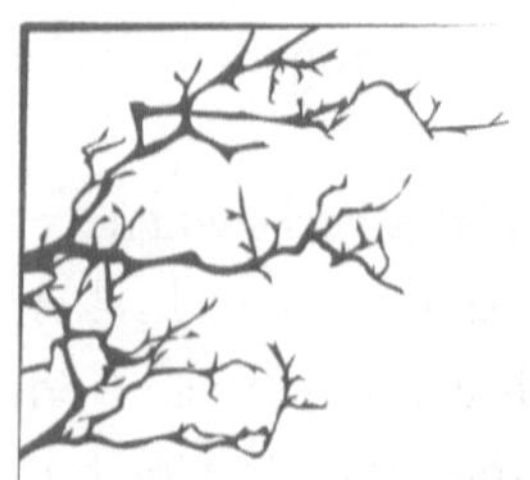

Chapter 8

Geson said nothing and soon recovered his usual self-possession. He asked Uncle Mute to wheel him into the study and then he closed the door. Gem stood there for a while before he returned to his room. The wedding night passed silently. Birds started to sing in the clear sky the next morning.

A middle-aged woman, who used to sell syrup-poached eggs at the back door of the mansion of the Fores, once told Sanbor that she had been at the mercy of her mother-in-law and that she would not have been able to cope with the harsh situation if she had not been helped by her husband. Her narration of the miseries of being a daughter-in-law made him shudder. That was what Sanbor had heard before his young master married Geson. A marriage in an ordinary family was so hard, to say nothing of living in such a big family as the Fangs. Would Geson support Gem? Sanbor was teeming with worry when he, holding dozens of eggs bought from the woman who had had painful memories, was thinking about what to do next.

So, now he was holding a club with his left hand and a knife with his right hand, which frightened the yawning Gem.

"Oh, what are you going to do, Sanbor?" he asked.

"To serve tea for the elders."

"What?"

"That's what a bride should do after the wedding night."

"I would rather pour the tea in the graveyard," Gem blurted out, glancing at the hemline of a dress of a woman who was eavesdropping on him at the door of the courtyard.

Sanbor thought that made sense, but a strong smell of smoke assailed his nostrils as soon as he threw away the club. Uncle Mute with a dusty face ran out of the kitchen in the east of the courtyard, holding a broken fan and coughing.

"What has happened?" Gem asked anxiously.

Uncle Mute bowed to Gem. The surname of the elderly man was Chou. He used to work as an accountant for the late Choron Fang.

"Did you cook just now?" Gem asked.

Uncle Mute gesticulated: "I'm sorry that I was a bad cook."

Gem shook his head. "Only you and Geson are living in this courtyard?" he added, holding his fan. "Where are the others?"

Uncle Mute looked sad but soon he smiled. He gesticulated: "You may rest now, and I'll go on to make breakfast. It'll be ready soon."

Gem and Sanbor entered the kitchen. A half-dead cock was put on the chopping board, a carp was jumping in a bucket, and the fragrant congee was still on the stove, which showed that the kitchen had been frequently used. Different from ordinary families, the Fangs were so demanding that they needed tasty cold appetisers, hot dishes, pastries, and sweet soup. Choron had been fastidious about food and tea, and his finely decorated kitchen had been comparable to that of in a high official's mansion. This place, however, was riddled with cobwebs and dust now. There was a large, clean, and much-used ceramic jar on the floor. Gem put down the fan and gave a quick death to the struggling chicken with the knife.

Gem had made futile attempts to find out what had happened to Geson, but he knew that Shrewdning Wong had been eager to lead the Fang family since Choron died.

Gem chopped chicken into small pieces and then asked Uncle Mute to get a pouch. The former stewed the meat together with the pouch full of thirteen kinds of herbs and fruits; after half an hour, he put some sauce into the pot.

"You are such a good cook, my young lord," Sanbor exclaimed in astonishment.

"My mother had stunning cooking skills," Gem replied, holding a large plate of appetising chicken. "I often watched her make meals, so gradually I could cook, too."

"But I've never seen your good skills in the kitchen, my young lord."

"You would have been jobless if I had been the cook."

"So let me finish the rest of the job," Sanbor said gladly.

Gem patted him on the shoulder and then went to the study, holding a plate of delicious meat and two bowls of congee with a lot of sugar in them.

Geson could not move at will and the door of the study was usually left ajar. He did not sleep in his room last night and today he asked Uncle Mute to put his quilts on a wooden couch behind the screen patterned with ink and wash paintings. He did not want to get close to Gem.

After Gem entered the study, he saw books on the desk and some impressive but unfinished Chinese characters on a piece of art paper: the writing brush had been stopped halfway and the strokes perhaps had been forgotten, leaving two drips of ink on the paper.

Geson was engrossed in reading a book that he did not hear the footsteps. Gem put the food down on the desk and then walked to the back of Geson as quietly as possible.

A stick of incense had been burning by half. "Would the scholar Liu be seduced by the female fox demon and lose all his energy and be late for the imperial competitive examination?" Gem asked.

It was a porno book in which a voluptuous nine-tailed fox demon was having hot sex with a handsome scholar. Gem was attracted by it and then he put his left hand on the back of Geson's wheelchair and lowered himself to the desk and turned a page for the avid reader.

"Oh, the poker-faced Mr. Geson Fang is devouring erotica," Gem said smilingly.

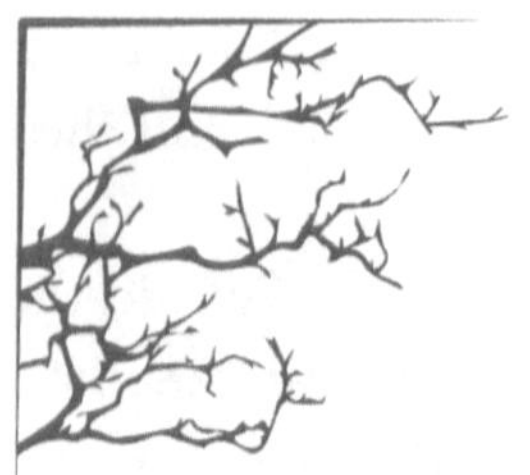

Chapter 9

Geson was a little surprised but soon he closed the book calmly. Gem pulled a chair and sat in it by the desk after he leant over Geson's ear for a while. The two men were seated face to face silently.

"Why did you come here?" Geson asked lightly, wearing his hair loose and a black cloak.

"Well, old friends should have had a nice chat," Gem replied.

"We were just acquaintances and we don't need to talk too much," Geson said coldly.

He seemed to have forgotten his happy days with Gem in childhood. Such unfriendliness would have made others walk away at once. Gem was still smiling at him after he gave Geson a pair of chopsticks which were not taken, so he put them down on the table.

The congee with shredded chicken was delicious. Gem had acquired a taste for putting sugar into his meals while Geson remained aloof.

"The Taos invited guests from the well-known families to the tea tasting event held by them in Yichou the year before last," Gem said. "Lady Rachel took me there and later I went to the Wonderful Alley with the grandson of the Taos. You must have been to that place which was renowned for palatable wine and tea, and for a beautiful woman's enchanting singing in a boat. Oh, I came across an interesting thing."

Geson looked at him dispassionately and wondered when he would leave.

"There was a fierce competition on tea art and the winner would spend the night with the captivating singer," Gem continued. "The tea house owners far and near scrambled for the hard-to-get chance. The tea bricks were not good enough but the water was said to have been fetched from remote, distinctive mountains. After different kinds of tea were boiled, the tastes of all of them turned out to be insipid and nobody could distinguish whether the water had come from mountains or wells. Someone broke a deadlock by saying that one of the special mountains was the source of the river outside. The river water right before their eyes would be the key to being the winner. So, hundreds of men jumped into the river, which frightened away the charming singer."

Mountain spring water was the best to brew tea, river water the second, and well water the last but it was often used by ordinary families. The quality of tea was important but there were two crucial factors on a tea tasting event: one was the duration of the white foam, which came after rapid agitation of tea with a bamboo whisk, staying on the inner surface of a cup after the tea was brewed; and the other one, which would decide the final result, was the tea liquid: fresh white foam would be superior and clear light yellow be common – the difference was closely related to water.

"But few people can produce the tea liquid covered with fresh white foam nowadays," Gem prattled, "even the Taos and the Hus can't ..."

"You can go now if you finish your talk," Geson interrupted.

Gem had to go. Later Uncle Mute entered the room and was stopped by Geson before he wanted to clear away the plates.

"You have heard our talk," the young master said.

Uncle Mute had been serving him for many years and understood him, so he nodded.

"He took me to Yichou but I drove him away," Geson said, lowering his head and watching his legs. "I wish that he would leave because I don't want to get him involved into the troubles of my family."

"Why are you in such a hurry, my young lord?" Sanbor asked outside. Geson could not hear the answer clearly inside but he thought that he had annoyed Gem.

Geson calmly opened the lock box in which he put a half piece of white jade the other day. Before he could take it out of the box, he heard someone kicking open the door of the study. He knew who the comer was. He put the box away so hastily that he heard a sharp clatter of the jade and he was worried whether the jade was still intact. He could not check on it but had to grasp the lid. Soon he saw Gem walking into the study, carrying a bundle wrapped in cloth on his shoulder, holding a quilt in his arms, and humming a tune.

"Why do you come back?" Geson asked.

"What are you hiding?" Gem retorted.

"Nothing," Geson replied imperturbably, moving his hands. "I can let Uncle Mute accompany you if you want to return to Jorleen, and I can give you sufficient money for the long journey."

"Are you caring about me?" Gem asked smilingly, putting his arms upon the quilt on the desk.

Geson tried to keep cool when he was pinching his own thighs as hard as he could, and then he looked away.

Meanwhile, Gem was happy to see that the congee had been had. He threw his quilt onto the wooden couch behind the screen and lay down.

"I asked you to return," Geson said, frowning.

"You are my husband now. You sleep in the study and I'm here with you," Gem said, pillowing his own head, with one leg upon the other.

"You ..." Geson wanted to let Gem go but did not know how, and soon he saw the latter walk up to him. "You are my husband now, and I should be with you," the spouse said.

Gem looked at a pair of golden orioles outside and said that they were a couple. He spent the whole morning having fun in the study and turned a deaf ear to Geson's mask of nonchalance.

Sanbor was sadly standing in the large courtyard in which only he and Gem together with Geson and Uncle Mute were living. The wedding ceremony yesterday was so coldly received by the Fang family that even a servant did not give a hoot about it. Sanbor anxiously tried to communicate with Uncle Mute but the former could neither understand the gestures nor the words written down on the ground by the latter with a branch.

The birds flied away and Gem caught sight of the words on the ground written by Uncle Mute.

"A serious fire broke out in the third year of the reign Goodpeace," Sanbor read out with difficulty. "Had your throat been destroyed by the heavy smoke?" he asked in astonishment. Uncle Mute nodded.

Gem knew about the fire which killed Choron Fang and his wife Orchid eight years ago. That day they took their son Geson to the fresh tea storehouse to make an inventory, but the dryness in hot weather made the things have spontaneous combustion. The boy lost his parents and lost his legs as a result of heavy loads falling from the beam. Geson was born into a family of tea production and he could recognise tea at the age of one, distinguish various tastes of it at the age of two, speculate about hundreds of species on tea tasting events and tell the name of each kind and its production method at the age of five. He might be proud sometimes but he used to be spirited. He should have managed the business of the Fangs and should have made his family become No. 1 among the four well-known ones. But now he was a puppet leader in a wheelchair.

Gem, leaning on the windowsill and holding a fan, considered that the fire had been too strange. Choron had been a trader of fresh tea. Green and moist tea buds would be made into a tea brick through dozens of processes, such as deactivation of enzymes, kneading, drying, compression, and carving. Before the bricks were produced, the fresh buds sent by tenant farmers would be put in storehouses, and the buds would not burn even in hot weather, to say nothing of trapping people. The accident was just an excuse and the reason had been only known by the arsonist who must have been a shrewd, cunning person in Gem's opinion.

The door of the study was opened. Gem and Geson saw a woman enter. She was Lady Shrewdning, the chief witness at the wedding ceremony yesterday.

"Wheel me to the drawing room, Gem," Geson said calmly, putting the book down.

Tea was served.

"Have your legs hurt during the rainy days, Geson?" Lady Shrewdning asked insincerely.

"I've been unable to feel any pain, auntie," Geson replied humbly. "But thanks for asking."

"I hope that you will regain good health as soon as possible," she added hypocritically. "Let Doctor Chen treat you again."

"OK," Geson said meekly.

"I'll have him come here tomorrow," she said. She asked a maid to bring a stool to Gem when she saw him standing behind Geson's wheelchair. Gem realised that she must have colluded with Lady Willow. He wanted to sit down but he was stopped by Geson, so he had to keep standing.

"How have your father and Lady Rachel been?" she asked, holding a tea cup.

"They are fine, my lady." Gem replied. "You are such a considerate businesswoman."

"Oh," Lady Shrewdning said in surprise, her little finger moving a bit while holding the lid of her tea cup. She had a faint smile on her face and then put down the cup on the table.

"What?" Gem asked.

"Well, the word businesswoman has been seldom mentioned in these years," she said.

"Lady Rachel has told me quite a lot about you that you were a wise businesswoman," Gem added. "Before I came here, Her Ladyship asked me to let Geson follow your example and make the tea trade prosper."

"I'm flattered," Lady Shrewdning said with an affected smile. "Lady Rachel is thoughtful and competent."

"I'm a new comer here and I'm trying to obey the rules of the Fangs," Gem said politely.

"Your husband is the head of the Fangs, Gem," she continued, glancing at Geson. "And I hope that you will help him manage the family affairs."

"You have done quite a lot for our family, auntie," Geson said. "Our business would have gone belly-up if you had not contributed to it." He wanted to end the conversation between Gem and the woman.

"I appreciate it," she said lightly. "By the way, give the account book to Geson, Amy."

Amy did that unwillingly after a moment of hesitation.

"About what?"

"The prefecture chief Lord Feng has placed an order for 5,000 tea bricks and hundreds of new pieces of our tea brand Lotusherb. He will share the bricks with his colleagues and give the Lotusherb to the powerful officials in the capital city as presents for better connections after he goes there in the next few days."

Geson flipped through it and returned it to Amy. "You will handle it, auntie," he said carelessly.

"But I should let you know about the details of our family business because you are the leader," Lady Shrewdning said with a silver tongue.

"I believe that you can do it well," Geson said.

"Really?" she asked with a teasing smile, fiddling with the lid of her tea cup.

"Yes."

"OK," she said. "You should have a good rest now and I'll visit you another day."

Gem wanted to follow her after she left, but he was stopped by Geson at once. "Don't worry," Gem whispered, holding his husband's wrist.

It was warm at noon. Gem walked with Lady Shrewdning until they got to the courtyard entrance. "You are a brilliant young man, Gem," she remarked. "And your capabilities to recognise different kinds of tea are comparable to Geson's."

"He outshines me," he replied humbly, his hands behind his back playing with his fan.

"Your father should have discovered your talent."

"He is just a farmer and not as wise as you, my lady."

"He is so extraordinary that he has been able to satisfy his two wives and make the Fores become one of the four well-known families with the help of his father-in-law," she said calmly, looking at him with her sharp eyes.

Shangyee was a smart man and his son Gem, who had been playing dumb for so many years, must be a deep card.

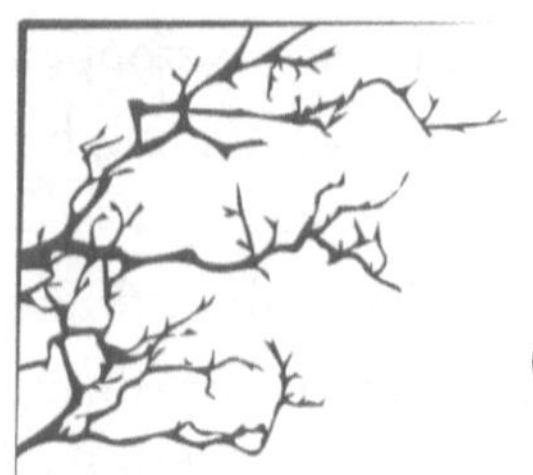

Chapter 10

Gem said nothing but saw Lady Shrewdning out. Just after he returned to the room, he found that Geson was staring at the back of the hand with which he stopped Gem from getting close to Lady Shrewdning when they met with her half an hour ago.

"What would you like to have for lunch?" Gem asked smilingly. Geson pretended to ignore him and called Uncle Mute and then he started to read a book. The couple had lunch and supper together.

Gem felt bored in the study and told Uncle Mute that he would go to the night market with Sanbor and would come back before bedtime.

The middle-aged man smiled at him and then he cleared away the plates and poured warm water into a bathtub. Geson took off his clothes and slowly sat in the bathtub with the help of Uncle Mute. His legs were riddled with scars.

The aroma of herbal medicine was permeating the air. Uncle Mute was stopped by Geson before he put the bag of medicine into the bathtub.

"Put it away," Geson said. "Doctor Chen will treat me tomorrow."

Fu Chen, who was the excellent Doctor Chen mentioned by Lady Shrewdning and had been running a clinic in downtown

Chuchou, failed to make Geson's legs return to normal although the therapy had been going on for many years. With trembling hands Uncle Mute went down on his knees and made mournful sounds.

"Don't worry," Geson said quietly, looking at him.

Uncle Mute nodded on the verge of tears and gesticulated if he would let Gem stay in the Fang family. Geson, lowering his head and watching his legs, shook his head.

The dazzling night market in the Gintang Street was comparable to that of in the Prosperity Street in Yichou or the Felicity Street in Jorleen. There was no curfew and thus the market was much livelier than in the daytime. A lot of pastries such as sugar-moulded minifigures and glazed fruits were tantalizing. Sanbor was less homesick when he was eating red bean cakes happily.

Gem walked to the end of the Street and stopped. "More sweetmeats?" he asked.

"I'm full, my young lord," Sanbor replied, swallowing the cakes. "Shall we return now?"

Gem looked at the moon and then put one tael of silver on the trolley selling lanterns. "Let's go now," he said.

There were sounds in the courtyard at 10 p.m. Geson had turned off the light and Gem's quilt had been carried to the main room by Uncle Mute. It was bedtime. Gem did not enter the study or the room after he came back.

Geson lying in the couch frowned at the sound of the rattles outside and called Uncle Mute but got no reply. Gem opened the door after one hour and walked in.

"I know you are still awake, Geson," he said smilingly, holding a lantern.

Geson watched him for a while and then closed his eyes. "I'll go to sleep right now," he said lightly.

Gem laughed and suddenly he leaned over Geson and took him firmly by the back and helped him sit up.

"What are you doing?" he exclaimed in surprise, trying to free himself from Gem's hands. "Let go of me!"

From behind Gem clasped the upper body of Geson who would be a tall, strong man if he could stand up. His mask of coldness started to crack while Gem put him into the wheelchair with difficulty. Both of them were panting. Gem put a coat on Geson's body before the latter could ask a question, and then the former wheeled him to the door and opened it.

A narrow path was made in the courtyard and it was flanked by many things when insects were chirping. What Geson could see now was the dim shadows of lanterns in the air. Gem clapped his hands and soon Sanbor and Uncle Mute lit up the lanterns.

The courtyard was glittering in the colourful lanterns. There was a vendor's trolley under each lantern and there were various kinds of interesting things, such as sweetmeats, pinwheels, masks, sugar-moulded minifigures including an unfinished one with a pout, and a fortune-teller's long narrow flag.

"Why did you do this?" Geson asked with sparkling eyes, grasping the wheelchair.

"Because tonight was so wonderful that I made the Gintang Street in miniature in this courtyard," Gem replied happily, walking up to him. "Now I can enjoy the moon with you."

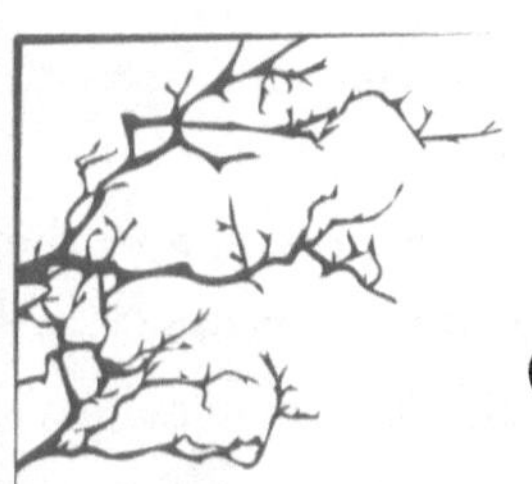

Chapter 11

Amy entered the room of Lady Shrewdning who was removing makeup when the lights were still on in the courtyard at midnight. Her Ladyship took a spoonful of the superior bird's nest soup to make her throat feel better.

"Have things been finished in the courtyard?" she asked.

"Yes, my lady," Amy replied.

"What did Geson say and do?"

"He looked cold," the maid answered, squatting and massaging her master's legs. "But why did Gem try so hard to please Geson?"

Lady Shrewdning put down the spoon and opened a powder box jammed with letters rather than cosmetics.

"Human beings can't live without affections," Her Ladyship said. "Gem feels pity for Geson for the sake of their childhood friendship."

"But Gem has done too much!" Amy said.

"He will do much more," the master added.

"Now Gem is the spouse and the supporter of Geson," Amy whispered. "You should have refused Lady Willow's request of having Gem marry Geson. The family wealth may ..."

"Geson is always the head of the Fangs," Lady Shrewdning said calmly, glancing at her maid, "and I just help him to manage the family business."

"I agree with you, my lady. But what if Gem might assist Geson in usurping the property of the Fang family?"

"All by himself?" Her Ladyship exclaimed, walking to the bedside and unfolding the bed curtain, "Even Lady Willow can't deal with the crafty Gem on whom I should keep an eye. I gave my consent to the arranged marriage for better business between our two families. But Geson will refuse Gem's assistance even though the latter wants to do so."

"But why?" Amy asked.

"Geson has so strong self-esteem that he will never ask for help even when he falls on hard times," her master said, lying on the bed.

Amy tucked her master in and put the golden silk embroidered shoes patterned with peonies in place. "Does Geson know the truth about the fire which happened many years ago?" she ventured.

"He is so smart that he knows everything," Her Ladyship replied lightly, closing her eyes.

The maid gave up the question that "if Geson would take revenge", and then she considered that he and his servant Uncle Mute had to live a humble life so that he would secure the family business.

"He knows what I want although we have been living in a false appearance of harmony," Lady Shrewdning added sanctimoniously. "After he comes around to my thought, he will let me lead the Fang family, which will be much better than his unpleasant situation now."

The trolleys were still in the courtyard the next morning. Gem in light blue clothes got up from the couch in the study and stretched himself. He threw himself onto the couch after he wheeled Geson into the room last night, and he started to snore when his husband tried to wake him up. He had a sound sleep and did not open his eyes until 9 a.m.

In the drawing room Geson was greeting Fu Chen who was in his fifties and had a handlebar moustache. The doctor stood up as soon as he saw Gem walking in. "Good morning, sir," he said.

"Good morning, sir. Are you Doctor Chen?" Gem asked politely with clasped hands.

"Yes, I am."

"Have a seat please, doctor," Gem said. "How was your sleep last night, Geson?"

"Good," he replied calmly. He wanted to keep silent but he had to say something when he saw Gem smiling at him.

"Really?"

"Yes."

"I'll stay with you tonight again."

Geson failed to find an excuse to let Gem leave the room.

"I'll give you an acupuncture treatment, sir," Dr. Chen said smilingly.

Geson nodded.

"Have you had any feeling in your legs recently, sir?" Dr. Chen asked, pressing Geson's knees. "Painful?"

"No," he replied.

"Do they hurt?" the doctor asked again, pressing his patient's lower legs hard.

"No," he said.

"You haven't got better," the doctor said. "I'll give you an acupuncture treatment now and change the medical recipe for the bath of your legs."

"Thank you, doctor," Geson said, and then he started to read a book. Meanwhile, Gem was having tea quietly and thinking about how to make Geson smile again, but suddenly he saw Uncle Mute standing there, looking worried and clenching his fists.

Gem saw the doctor out after the latter finished the one-hour treatment.

"When will Geson's legs return to normal?" Gem asked.

"He should have regained his health," the doctor replied.

"What do you mean?"

"His legs had got hurt by the falling heavy objects. I had given him a physical examination and set his bones. He would have been able to walk after six-month rehabilitation, but he has been sitting in a wheelchair for eight years, which is strange."

"Has Geson been pretending to be paralysed?"

"No. I'm an experienced doctor and I can see that he can't stand up."

"Why are you so sure about it? He should have got better."

"Lady Shrewdning often asks me about it."

"Her Ladyship and you ..."

"I used to be a barefoot doctor in the hometown of Lady Shrewdning. Several years ago I was asked to treat Geson, and later I was required to stay in the city to give further treatment to him."

Lady Shrewdning had doubts about Geson's legs, so she had Dr. Chen work for her. Gem had never asked about Geson's illness and he would need to know more now.

"Have you found out the crux of Geson's problem?" Gem continued.

"I guess that it has had something to do with the fire which happened more than a decade ago in the Fang family," the doctor explained. "Since then Geson has been traumatised by it and has been unable to walk again."

"Really?"

"Yes. The acupuncture therapy can't cure his distress."

"Thank you very much, doctor," Gem said after a moment of silence. "This way please."

Gem went into the study and he knew that Geson would be there. He was right. Uncle Mute, looking calm with marks of teary eyes, smiled at Gem and gesticulated that he would make tea.

It was the Lesser Fullness of Grain in May. Gem was humming, teasing the golden carp in the white-jade aquarium, watering the pomegranate flowers in the pots and pruning. He was enjoying himself so much so that he seemed to forget that Geson was still in the study. Later he could feel that someone was watching him and then he sat opposite Geson and snatched the book from his hands.

Geson remained cool and started to read another book, but it was taken away by Gem at once before it could be opened.

"What are you doing?" Geson asked, sulking.

"Why did you watch me just now?" Gem retorted.

"I did not watch you."

"We are in our little world. Just do what you want."

Geson looked serious and took a third book.

Gem snatched it again. "Don't read the book," he said smilingly. "Look at me now."

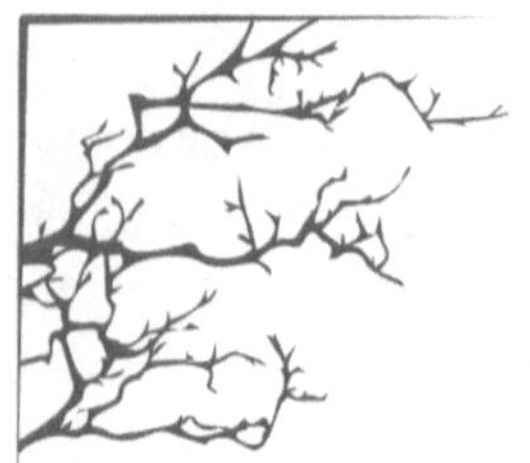

Chapter 12

What the doctor had said might be right. Geson had been in the limelight before he was fifteen. But he had been a victim of the disaster and had been living in the shadows of Lady Shrewdning's covetousness since the fire happened. He was the only son of the Fangs, and their relatives could not undermine the female leader of the family although they disliked her. The cunning, hypocritical woman, who had turned the family into her own turf through eight years, treated Geson insincerely and didn't care two hoots about his marriage.

Gem would not interfere in the family affairs of the Fangs but he could not figure out what Geson would do. He would not have racked his brains to marry Geson if the latter had not ignored him. Gem had always protected himself from being hurt by anybody since his childhood, but he would need to find if he was still in Geson's heart after the former had been missing him for so many years.

"You are getting too close to me."

"Huh?"

Gem asked Geson to look at him, so the former sat on his lap tenderly and put his forehead against that of the latter. When they were kids, they often shared a bed and talked about the interesting things they had seen during their travels, and they would think of ideas of how to lure Jack into a riverbank and push him downwards, and of how to help the little sister Lily climb a tree.

"Lily has eloped with her sweetheart," Gem said smilingly.

"I know that," Geson said calmly.

"She often chased after you and said that she would marry you after she grew up," Gem added. "But now she has fallen in love with another man."

"We were just children at that time," Geson replied lightly.

"Really? I remember that you had had a sweetheart, too," Gem said wittingly. He, putting his hands on the armrest of the wheelchair, pressed his forehead against Geson's so hard that the latter had to lean on the back of the wheelchair. Meanwhile, Geson blinked and moved his gaze from Gem's face to the ground.

"Tell me now," Gem whispered, putting his nose against Geson's, leaning forward and locking him into the wheelchair.

The same thing had been mentioned frequently in their childhood. The little girl Lily said that she liked Geson, while the two older boys had known much more than she had. Gem asked Geson of whom he had been fond, the latter, blushing and trying to keep calm, said that he would bring up proposal of marriage and have one terrific wedding after he grew up.

"When will that person reach the age of marriage?" Gem asked peevishly.

Geson held out three fingers.

"Three years later?" Gem exclaimed.

Geson nodded seriously.

"But life is so unpredictable that she may marry another man and have children three years later," Gem warned.

"My beloved one is a man," Geson said proudly.

"But he may marry a woman and become a father three years later," Gem remarked jealously, looking at his own chest. "I would not wait for you for three years if I were him, and I would meet a better person." He wanted to go but his wrist was grasped by Geson while the former was too annoyed to ask him why.

"Good things won't come easy," Geson said after a moment of silence.

Since then Gem had been tormented by futile waiting and expectation.

Now Gem saw Geson looking away but gripping the wheelchair, and then he heard Sanbor shouting excitedly outside before he could say something.

"Good news, my young lord!" Sanbor cried. "We have a visitor!"

Geson felt relieved at once and then Gem went leisurely out of the room holding a fan.

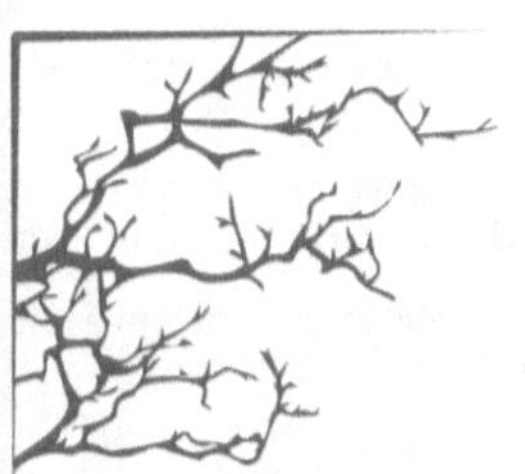

Chapter 13

A man came in. "Oh, that's Layman Tao!" The visitor in lavender clothes stumbled and almost fell at the sight of Gem.

"Mr. Tao!" Sanbor cried, supporting the guest to stand up.

The true name of the twenty-one-year-old comer was Adept Tao who was the grandson of the head of the Taos in Yichou and was named by his grandfather in the hope of becoming a wise, successful businessman in tea markets. In one tea tasting event, he was asked by the elders to recognise different kinds of tea but he gave wrong answers, and later he was nicknamed Layman by Gem. In spite of that, they were good friends.

"Oh, you have indeed married Geson, Gem!" Adept exclaimed in surprise. "It must be the scheme of Lady Willow to force you to do so!"

"What brings you here?" Gem asked curiously.

"The tea tasting event will be held in Chuchou this year," Adept replied. "My grandpa and I have got here ahead of schedule for business."

Gem realised that he had not taken part in such an event for many years. The reason, instead of Geson's absence, was that Lady Willow had replaced the sick Lady Rachel and used her invitation letters to join in the events with her own son Jack.

"Are you going to expand your family business in Chuchou?" Gem asked.

"We do business freely," Adept replied glibly. "The tea produced by my family has been much favoured and will be widely promoted."

"Since when has this place been chosen?" Gem asked smilingly.

Adept understood him. "Since Mr. Choron Fang passed away," he said in a tone of friendliness. "Lady Willow and Lady Shrewdning are jackals from the same lair. The former has been eying the wealth of the Fangs' business covetously for her own sons. The members in the Chamber of Commerce of the Tea (CCT) are hypocrites when they speak of Geson who had lost his parents, but become sharks when they scramble for the market shares."

Adept realised that he was standing in the courtyard of Geson's house after he stopped prattling. "Is Geson in?" he whispered, looking around.

"Yes, in the study," Gem replied.

"I haven't met him for nine years. Is he willing to see me?"

Uncle Mute wheeled Geson into the courtyard before Gem could say something.

"Oh, I haven't seen you for ages, Geson," Adept exclaimed in surprise after a moment of staring at him.

"Nice to see you again," Geson said politely with a nod. "Let's go to the drawing room."

When Adept was holding a white-jade cup patterned with swans and sipping the fresh tea, he glanced at Geson's legs and had to gulp down mouthfuls of tea to make himself less attentive to the man's lower limbs, and he belched after having three cups of tea. Meanwhile, Gem was watching his friend playfully instead of easing his embarrassment, which made the latter glare at the onlooker.

"How have you been in these years, Geson?" Adept ventured, putting down the cup on the table.

He immediately realised that he should not have asked such a stupid question, but Geson had Uncle Mute refill the guest's cup.

"I'm fine," Geson replied.

"That's good."

Adept knew that he had been outshone by Geson since childhood. The fire which had happened in the Fangs had acted as a trigger for sorrow and gloat, and their competitors had seized the market shares since Mr. Choron Fang passed away. Moreover, Lady Shrewdning had been so preoccupied with how to turn Geson into a puppet leader of the Fangs that she had failed to manage the family business well. The tea tasting event would be held in Chuchou this year, which meant that Lady Shrewdning had resumed the tea business and would have a say in the decisions of the relatives of the Fangs.

"Will you participate in the event to be held in Mount Yumin?" Adept asked.

Geson shook his head. "Who will be invited except the Big Four?" he said.

"It is said that a big shot from the capital city will join in the upcoming event," Adept replied.

Lady Shrewdning attached more importance to the connections with officials rather than less important tea traders. She had spent enormous amounts of money inviting an important personage to judge the event so that she would facilitate the sales of the tea brand which had been produced by the Fangs and operated by her in exalted circles.

Gem and Sanbor came back at 9:45 p.m. after they went to a restaurant for dinner with Adept. Gem holding a jar of osmanthus wine walked into the study in which Geson was wearing a large coat, leaning on the couch and playing chess by himself.

The ground was in a mess. When Gem saw the fragments of a square vase which was patterned with birds and flowers as a container for scroll paintings and which had been placed on a windowsill, he came to realise why Geson had been regarded as a lunatic.

He sat opposite Geson on the couch and joined him. He soon gained the upper hand but Geson was still engrossed in the game. The winner would be the one who could seize the opportunity; but if one step was wrong, the whole game would be a bungle.

"You should put your chess piece here," Gem said, clamping one piece with his two fingers and pointing at a blank area on the chessboard.

Geson remained silent, a lock of hair falling around his temples, and he avoided the position after a moment of hesitation.

Gem snatched the black chess piece from Geson's hand, and he had a black one and a white one in the centre of his palm.

"Does your chance come?" Gem asked.

Geson's eyes met Gem's. The latter could understand the former.

"You should seize the opportunity and take an easy path," Gem said. He put the black piece on the originally-chosen position of the chessboard and then placed the white one on the black one.

Geson silently held a new piece and touched it tenderly.

"You don't want to use it?" Gem asked teasingly, leaning forward.

Geson blinked and put the chess piece into the container. "You don't have to get involved in it," he replied lightly.

"But I'm willing to," Gem said with delight.

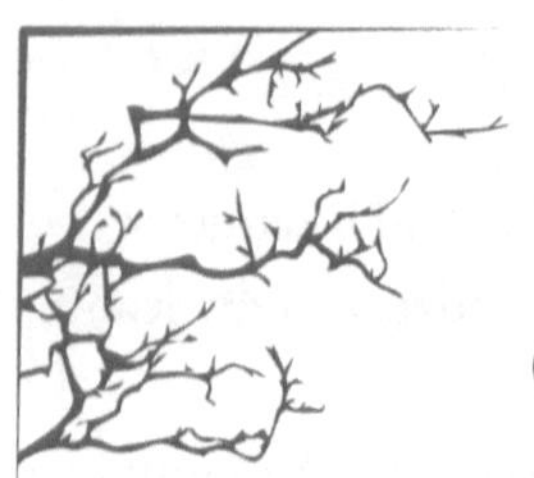

Chapter 14

Gem got drunk and with a sharp clatter he leaned over the chess table and fell asleep. Geson looked at him and then put the two chess pieces into the palm of his own hand. He slowly held out one of his arms over the table and put his head on it, watching Gem. The sleeping man looked lovely and started to talk, and Geson's ears pricked up.

"I had taken a long journey with my three shoes worn out and with a half-full stomach of cold steamed bread for two weeks, but you refused to see me when I was standing outside your house. You ..." Gem suddenly sat up with half-opened eyes. Geson thought that he had woken up but the man, pointing at the window, continued his speech tipsily, "You ... you ... had made me unhappy ..."

Gem was staring at the chess pieces and his head was held by Geson's hands just before it fell onto the chessboard. Meanwhile, Uncle Mute entered the study to change the wicks and saw Geson sitting at the chess table and protecting Gem's head from the chess pieces.

The elderly man gesticulated smilingly that Gem had got drunk. Geson, leaning on a square pillow, nodded. Uncle Mute continued with his gestures: "Gem has been fond of wine since childhood."

Gem was not a good drinker and preferred fruit wine to liquor. Lady Rachel asked him to have more tea instead of wine when he was a kid. Shangyee disliked alcohol and criticised that drinking would make trouble, so there was no jar of wine in the Fore family. Choron used to take Geson to visit the well-known families each year, and Gem hoped that his playmate would soon come to see him with delicious wine. Geson, in white clothes embroidered with golden silk, often held a jar of fruit wine and walked into the courtyard in which Gem was living. The two boys hid themselves behind a pear tree, and Geson watched Gem sipping the wine. The drinker looked forward that his buddy would bring more the next time, but the former often had such a massive hangover that the latter was too worried to let him have more.

Now Gem could indulge in the alcohol.

"Make sober-up tea tomorrow morning," Geson said.

The wick on the chess table was almost burnt out. Uncle Mute nodded and gesticulated if Gem would be sent to the main room. Geson gave a nod. Uncle Mute and Sanbor supported Gem into the main room.

Gem got up woozily and he did not become refreshed until he fumbled for a cup of ginseng tea near the bed and had it. Sanbor had made breakfast – a bowl of congee and two dishes – for his young master, and he had brewed another pot of ginseng tea and poured it into two cups. Gem stretched himself and glanced at the breakfast. He got dressed and washed up, gargled with tea, and then went to the study holding the breakfast and bamboo chopsticks.

It was nearly ten o'clock in the morning. Gem thought that Geson had had breakfast, but he met Uncle Mute at the door.

Gem smiled and entered the room, sat opposite his husband and tasted the dish made for the latter. Meanwhile, Geson remained poker-faced and seemed to forget what happened last night. Uncle Mute sighed and left after he made a futile attempt to gesticulate.

After the couple finished breakfast, Geson wheeled himself to the desk while Gem asked Sanbor to clear the table. Gem heard Geson calling his name before he wanted to have a nap. That was strange. Gem frowned and, holding a fan, walked towards him.

The desk was full of ink marks. Geson wrote a statement of divorce with a blackwood wolf-hair brush and then he gave it to Gem.

Gem held it and blow-dried the ink with his mouth. "Your offer may not be good news," he said smilingly.

"Our friendship had been gone," Geson said resolutely after a moment of silence. "Now everything is different from the past and we will be strangers."

Gem waggled the paper and then tore it up.

"Why did you do that?" Geson asked in surprise.

Gem threw away the pieces and leaned forward. "Do you think that I'm too drunken to remember the chess game last night?" he asked teasingly, raising Geson's chin with the fan.

"Is it still on your mind?"

"Yes," Gem replied lightly. "You said that you would not let me get involved. If you could have me stay with you, you would get a better result; but things might be different if I had to act recklessly."

"Is that a push?" Geson asked after a long moment of silence, curling his own fingers in the large sleeves.

"Are you willing to do it?" Gem smiled.

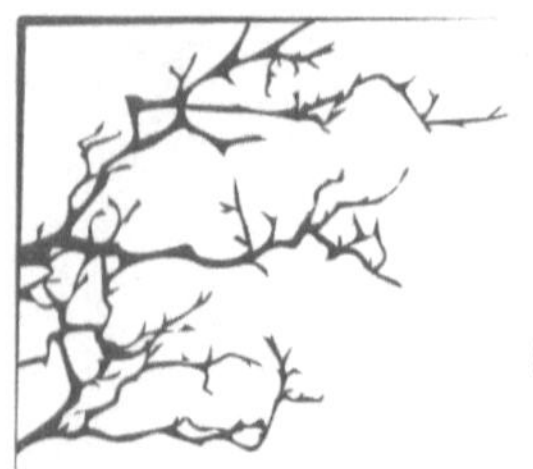

Chapter 15

Uncle Mute entered the room and saw Geson sitting at the desk and looking serious, ears with a red hue. With his hands trembling in the sleeves, Geson tried to subdue his anger. The elderly man gesticulated if his master had had a quarrel with Gem.

"I would not give a hoot about his choice," Geson said after a long moment of silence, blushing.

Uncle Mute looked at his master in puzzlement.

"That's what I should have told him," Geson added regretfully, frowning.

What had been said and done, however, would not be changed.

The tea tasting event would be held after half a month.

Adept had spent much time dealing with business and chatting with Gem and was staying in the mansion of the Fangs. Lady Shrewdning regarded Adept as an honoured guest, so she had the dirty, cobwebbed rooms cleaned and asked four men to serve him.

"Geson has been avoiding the society of others since the fire happened and I have to leave him alone," Lady Shrewdning said, wearing a long, lavender dress embroidered with clouds and lotuses, holding a white porcelain cup and sitting in the main position of the drawing room. "You are a guest here, Adept. I hope that you and Gem will cheer him up so that I can let him run the family business."

Adept, whose azure blue robe was outshining Gem's light green one, put down the tea cup and stood up. "Don't worry, my lady," he said reverently. "I have been one of Geson's friends since childhood, and I will persuade him to stage a comeback."

Lady Shrewdning used a silk handkerchief to wipe away her crocodile tears. "Enjoy your stay here, Adept," she said.

The young man tried to look sad but rolled his eyes as soon as the woman left. He asked the four servants to pack up and then he played chess with Gem under an osmanthus tree.

It was early summer with warm breezes. Carps were swimming in a lotus pond full of clear water.

"Who will be invited by Lady Shrewdning as the judge of the tea tasting event?" Adept asked, putting a black chess piece on the chessboard.

Gem made a move on the chessboard after a moment of silence. "An official," he replied.

"I know that," Adept said. He put another piece on the chessboard after a long moment of hesitation. "But what's his position in the government? She is eager to get into the tea markets now but she has few supporters and she will not be helped by the relatives of the Fangs. The other three influential families together with the Chaos, the Lins, the Weys, and the Chens, are vultures. She has been managing the business of the Fangs for so many years, but she won't gain a place in the tea markets if she can't be assisted by an imperial official."

Gem watched the chessboard, yawned lazily and messed up Adept's plan. "The judge is an imperial official," he said lightly.

"But how has she done it?" Adept asked in puzzlement.

"She is shrewd and cunning," Gem replied, having a mouthful of tea.

"You don't hit the nail on the head and you are not interested in the tea markets. Let's end the game. Shall we go for a drink?"

Adept was instructed to be a businessman although he was a hedonist. Now he just wanted to have fun with his friend.

Gem glanced at the study with closed doors and windows and then he went outside together with Adept and Sanbor.

Gem started to eat alone and avoided the study and spent much time outside the house. He came back very late tonight and saw the candlelight flickering in the study as soon as he entered the courtyard, but the light went out quickly. Holding a fan and humming a merry little tune, he went into the main room to sleep. The next morning he and Adept went to the market to buy canaries.

It was midnight but Gem had not come home. The light was still on in the study. Geson was writing at his desk while he was distracted by the noises outside and the two fighting crickets, but soon he was attracted by the night breeze and tree rustling. He frowned and wanted to look outside, but something on his mind made him blow out the candle. He wheeled himself towards the window which was ajar under the moonlight. He could not see the courtyard clearly, so he moved his wheelchair forward for a closer look.

He found no trace of the man he wanted to see and he frowned much more. He intended to wait for him in the dark but soon he heard rustles from the corner of a wall. Suddenly he caught sight of a man wearing a white-jade hairpin. That man was Gem who had spent a whole day outside the mansion.

"Are you looking for me?" Gem smiled.

"When did you return?" Geson asked in surprise.

"Just before you turned off the light," Gem replied, leaning on the windowsill and holding a fan. He often came back chatting with Adept but he returned alone tonight.

Geson perceived his trick. "Adept was not with you?" he asked.

"He will stay overnight in another place."

"Where is Sanbor?" Geson asked, looking at the dark main room.

"They are still waiting for me in a pub," Gem said teasingly. "I tell you that I'll spend the night somewhere else lest you should be worried about me."

"What?" Geson asked in astonishment.

"I'll keep drinking until I vomit and faint," the other man responded invitingly, holding his own chin with one hand.

"You ... you are ... not with me. How ... how can I ... ensure your safety?" Geson stammered after a moment of hesitation, looking away.

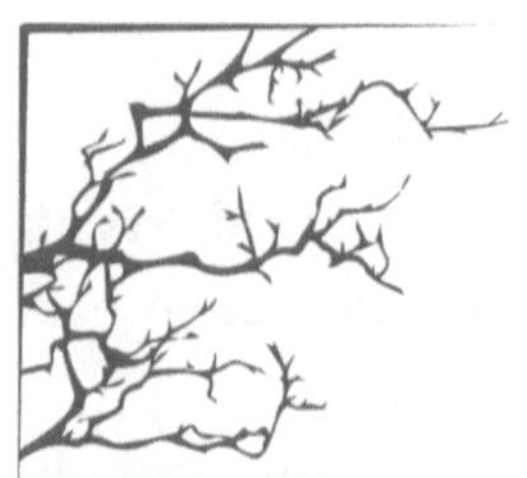

Chapter 16

Chuchou was teeming with people and carriages. Two new crossing points had been set up within several nights to smooth traffic flow. Hotels and restaurants were packed with customers and even some pretty boys and girls had to work as servants. The tea tasting event would be held in Mount Yumin after so many years had passed, and the ceremony would attract a large number of tea traders and poets.

Lady Shrewdning had been too preoccupied with the event to manage the guest rooms in the outer chambers. She had had four servants take good care of Adept and keep an eye on Geson. Even Adept could guess what she wanted to do and such a clever man as Geson could, too. The puppet leader of the Fangs had been living like a hermit and sometimes might be unstable and moody, but the paranoid woman had been staying alert. She had never let her guard down on anybody or anything, and she would keep a close watch on Geson even though he was a cripple.

"How is it going in the inner chambers?" Lady Shrewdning asked.

"Adept and Gem have spent much time enjoying themselves outside the mansion," Amy replied frankly.

"How about Geson?"

"He remains unsociable. The other day he lost his temper, smashed a vase and tore up several picture scrolls, and he seemed to have had a quarrel with Gem. The latter slept in the study with Geson several days ago, but now he sleeps in the main room alone. The two men are indifferent to each other."

"Gem has such high self-esteem that he can't endure Geson's apathy in spite of their deep childhood friendship," the female master said, brushing the warm tea with the cup lid.

"Don't worry, my lady. I'll keep a lookout for the inner chambers and things won't go amiss."

The lady nodded and went into the bedroom. She took several letters out of a drawer and flipped through them. She had been familiar with the content but now she read them again.

"When will the Fores get here?" she asked.

"Just before the tea tasting event begins," her maid replied.

"Has the invitation been received by Lady Rachel?"

"By Lady Willow."

Lady Shrewdning smirked and put away the letters. "Something interesting is coming," she said.

The female manager got busier when the event was getting closer. In order to deal with business easily, she chose to live nearby the Yunho House in Changping Street. The House was the best restaurant in the city and was also a part of the revenues of the Fangs.

Meanwhile, the servants of the Fang family became idlers who did not open the gate until it was afternoon and just ignored Geson. Whenever Amy came to the inner chambers, she either saw Gem and Adept play chess in the courtyard or Geson sit alone in a trance in the study. What's more, he would pay no attention to Gem if the latter tried to speak to him, and would shut the door if he was invited by Adept to go out. Those things bored her stiff. She was the trusted maid of Lady Shrewdning, but she could not help thinking that Her Ladyship had been overly-suspicious of Geson who might stand up someday and become the true head of the Fangs.

Amy brought cakes and pastries to the inner chambers and asked the servants what was going on. She returned to the outer chambers after she was told that Geson had remained the same.

Adept would go out today and wanted to be accompanied by Gem, but he saw the latter walking out of the room weakly supported by Sanbor with his hands. "What has happened?" he asked.

Gem did not speak but gave a sign to his servant. "My young master has had a fever and he must have a good rest," Sanbor said loudly.

"He is in need of a doctor now," Adept said.

"Medicine rather than a doctor has been able to make him get better soon ever since his childhood," Sanbor added.

"Buy medicine at once," Adept said.

Sanbor looked at the four servants and showed Adept a prescription. The medicine would be bought in four different pharmacies across the city. Sanbor could not finish the task by himself within one day.

Adept glanced at the prescription and realised that he used to take some of the pills when he had a fever. But two kinds of medicine on the prescription would be hard to get. He asked one of the four servants to write three copies of the original one. They each had one copy but did not know what to do.

"Do it now," Adept snapped.

The servants looked at the patient and went to buy medicine at once.

"You are seriously ill now and you must be treated by a doctor," Adept said, putting one hand on Gem's forehead.

Gem thanked him for his help. Adept asked Sanbor to look after his young master and then he went to call a doctor. Sanbor assisted Gem into the bedroom.

The rolling of a wheelchair broke the quietness of the room. Sanbor had left and Gem was lying on the bed, closing his eyes.

Geson looked calm. Uncle Mute wheeled him beside the bed and then touched Gem's forehead and immediately gesticulated: "Gem is in a dire situation."

Geson frowned and, glancing at a basin of used warm water, asked Uncle Mute to bring a new one. "You should get up now, Gem," he said.

Gem remained motionless, coughing and moaning in pain with his hands trembling. Geson was so worried about him that he wheeled himself closer to the bed. "Elder brother ..." Gem murmured.

That made Geson's heart thud. Gem, six months younger than him, used to call him "elder brother" when they were just little kids. Geson was happy to hear that because he had no siblings. As he grew up, however, what he wanted was more than being a brother.

His whispers attracted Geson to move closer to his body. He touched Gem's cheeks tenderly and silently for a while.

"My dear Gem," Geson said softly.

Birds were chirping outside the window and two canaries were peeping into the room. With his eyes closed Gem seemed to hear that and smiled serenely. Geson blushed at once and tried to leave, but he was grasped by the man lying on the bed.

To be continue......

Did you love *Gem & Geson: Meet Again*? Then you should read *Spring in the Shabby Lane*[1] by MODERCANTA!

Joseph and George were once university classmates. Back then, Joseph was the prodigal sun, shining brightly for all to see, while George was but a commonplace student. In a twist of fate, George stumbled upon a fragment of a photograph featuring Joseph. From that moment, a silent, one-sided love was kindled, a flame that would burn quietly for a decade.

---

1. https://books2read.com/u/49dEEY

2. https://books2read.com/u/49dEEY

Also by Sweet One

Gem & Geson
Gem & Geson: Meet Again
Gem & Geson: Become the True Leader of the Fangs
Gem & Geson: Always Be Together
Gem & Geson